Printed in the United States of America

First Printing 2018

ISBN 978-1-944644-03-1

Library of Congress Control Number: 2017956646

Juvenile Fiction – Mermaids

Social Themes - New Experience/Friendship

Crimson Dragon Publishing

4255 S Buckley Rd, #405

Aurora, Colorado 80013-2951

www.crimsondragonpublishing.com

a mermaid named Pearl is bored in her pet shop tank.

A sweet, young girl is looking for a pet to call her own.

Seeing the young girl, Pearl sings, "Oh please adopt me!"

Whisking away from her dull tank,

Pearl sets off for a new home.

Once at her new home,

"Weee!" Pearl cheers happily.

"Look out below," Pearl says as she swims to her new friend.

"It's treasure," the two sing.

Pearl dreams of wearing a pretty crown and sparkly gems.

Jelly grabs Pearl's hand and both shout, "Let's go!"

Pearl can float to the treasure in a bubble!

"Just keep trying," Jelly encourages as Pearl swims into another bubble.

Bead by bead, Pearl climbs up a pretty necklace lying outside the treasure box.

"It is even prettier up close," Pearl sings happily.

Pearl dives into the sparkling waves of jewels and gems.

While playing with her pretty treasure, Pearl hears a soft giggle.

Pearl pops her petite head from the treasure box and sees the little girl!

Sugary sweets and twinkling stardust create the collection of fantasies from the mind of illustrator, Amber Heaton. Amber has her Bachelor's degree in illustration from Kendall College of Art and Design in Grand Rapids, MI. When Amber isn't dreaming in pink, she's snuggling up with her kitties and watching horror movies. She is pursuing her dreams of becoming a children's book illustrator and wedding stationery designer while also working in production art.